Fireman Sam

Fireman Sam's Favourite Tales

EGMONT
We bring stories to life

First published in Great Britain 2011 by Egmont UK Limited
239 Kensington High Street, London W8 6SA

ISBN 978 1 4052 6177 7
50931/1
Printed in Italy

Contents

6   The Pontypandy Flood

When a flood hits Pontypandy, it's up to Fireman Sam and his team to keep everyone safe. But when Norman goes to save his pet sheep, will he be the one in danger?

34   Hot Dog

Mandy is sure that Radar, the Fire Station dog, would make a great sniffer dog, but her dad Mike isn't so sure. So when Mike has an accident, Radar has the chance to prove he can be a hero!

64   Plane Crazy

Naughty Norman Price has been making paper aeroplanes, and when one of his planes crash-lands in the Fire Station kitchen, Sam and the crew must fight a fire much closer to home!

92   The Hero Next Door

Sam decides to take a well-deserved day off from the Fire Station, but a series of disasters in Pontypandy reminds him that good firefighters are never off duty!

122   The Great Fire of Pontypandy

When a raging fire threatens Pontypandy, it's Fireman Sam and his crew to the rescue!

THE PONTYPANDY FLOOD

It was a beautiful morning in Pontypandy. The sun was shining, the birds were singing and in his bedroom over his mum's shop, Norman Price had just woken up.

Norman hated getting up early. He yawned and stretched as he pulled on his clothes, before shuffling over to his bedroom window.

When he pulled the curtains apart, Norman couldn't believe what he saw. Charlie's fishing boat was outside his bedroom window!

Norman ran downstairs to find his mum standing on the shop counter with water all around. "Mam!" he told her, "I think the whole town is flooded!"

Dilys thought for a moment. "You'd better get back upstairs," she said. "I'll ring the Fire Station to find out what to do."

But Norman had other things on his mind. "Do you think Woolly and Lambikins will be all right in their field?" Norman asked.

"I'm sure they'll be fine," Dilys said as she searched a shelf for her mobile phone.

Meanwhile, up in Wallaby One, Fireman Sam and Tom Thomas were flying across Pontypandy, looking down at the damage.

"This is the worst high tide I've ever seen," Sam told Tom.

Just then, Wallaby One's radio crackled and Station Officer Steele's voice boomed out.

"The Jones family went onto their roof to escape the flood," he said. "Now they are stuck and need help getting to safety."

"We're on our way, Sir!" Sam replied as Tom steered Wallaby One towards the Quayside.

11

When they arrived at the Wholefish Café, Sam bravely lowered himself down from Wallaby One in a special harness.

"Is everyone all right?" Sam asked.

"We're OK," Bronwyn replied. "But we can't find Lion!"

"I'm sure he'll be fine – he's a clever cat," said Sam. "Let's get you all back to the station."

And so, one by one, Sam winched the Jones family to safety.

At the same time, Penny and Elvis were steering Neptune through the flooded streets to help anyone in need. They found Trevor stranded on top of his bus.

"I'm glad to see you!" Trevor said as he wriggled down and landed softly on board Neptune. The three of them set off towards the safety of the Fire Station.

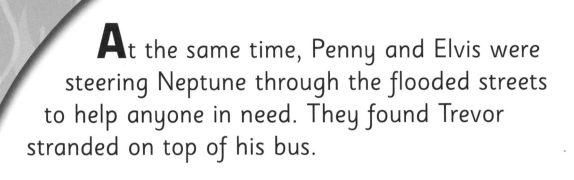

Back in his bedroom, Norman was still worried about Woolly and Lambikins.

As he gazed out of his window towards their field, something caught his eye. A small rowing boat had drifted under his window. Norman looked at it for a moment and an idea popped into his head.

"I'll go to the field and save them myself!" he said aloud. Soon he was shimmying down a rope made of knotted bedsheets, into the boat.

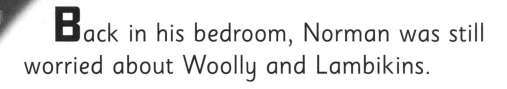

As Norman rowed the boat through Pontypandy, he heard a noise.

Meow! Norman stopped rowing ...

Meow! There it was again ...

Meow! Norman looked around and saw Lion floating on an upturned dustbin lid. He helped the poor little cat into his boat, and then he set off to save Woolly and Lambikins.

Penny, Elvis and Trevor were sailing past the shop in Neptune when Dilys rushed out. "Help!" she called. "Norman's disappeared!"

In a panic, Trevor jumped down from Neptune. "Don't worry, Dilys!" he said. "I'm here to help!"

But Dilys wasn't listening. "He was worried about Woolly and Lambikins," she told Penny and Elvis. "I think he may have gone to save them!"

"We need to talk to Wallaby One!" gasped Penny as she grabbed the lifeboat's radio. "Penny to Sam ... do you hear me?"

In Wallaby One, Sam and Tom were back in the air after dropping the Jones family at the Fire Station. "Reading you loud and clear, Penny. What's the problem?"

"Norman has gone out alone in the flood water to look for his sheep," Penny said over the radio.

"OK, Penny, we'll start a search operation from up here while you and Elvis search from Neptune," Sam said calmly.

And with that, Tom swooped Wallaby One back over the town and towards the fields.

Back in his rowing boat, Norman had finally found Woolly and Lambikins and pulled the two sheep into the boat. But the little lamb was scared and wouldn't stop rushing around. The boat began to rock and sway ...

"Stay still, Lambikins!" Norman said as he reached for his oars. But his weight unbalanced the boat even more and he toppled overboard!

Splash!

Norman splashed around in the cold water.

"Help!" he shouted as loudly as he could, but there was no one around to hear him. As he thrashed around in the water, the boat began to drift away from him, taking Woolly, Lambikins and Lion with it.

Up in Wallaby One, Sam and Tom were zooming across the bay when they saw something below. It was Norman!

Sam grabbed the radio. "Sam to Penny," he said. "Norman is in the water at Breaker's Field. This is an emergency!"

"Penny to Sam," came her reply. "We'll get there straight away!"

Back in Neptune, Elvis and Dilys held on tightly as Penny cranked the lifeboat's engine up to full speed. Soon they were skimming across the water towards Breaker's Field.

When they saw Norman, Penny slowed down before Elvis pulled him out of the water.

"It's a good job you're wearing your lifejacket, Norman," said Penny.

"Thanks for saving me," he replied. "But we need to get Woolly, Lambikins and Lion, too!" The animals were still floating out to sea!

Penny whizzed to the rescue! The animals were very scared, but Norman spoke to them softly as Penny gently lifted them into the lifeboat. They were safe at last!

Back at the Fire Station, everyone was
pleased to see Norman and the animals safe
and well. The tide was going out, and the
flood waters were going down.

"You shouldn't have gone out in the flood,"
Station Officer Steele told Norman sternly.
"You were in real danger out there."

"But you were very brave for saving the animals,"
Fireman Sam said, kindly, "even if we had to save
you in the end!"

HOT DOG

It was early morning. Mike Flood had lots of jobs to do, starting at the Fire Station. Mandy liked visiting the Fire Station – she especially liked Radar, the station dog.

"I don't even know why they have a dog at a Fire Station," said Mike.

"He's a rescue dog, Dad!" Mandy argued.

"He's a pet, Mandy!" Mike replied.

Mandy's mum, Helen, came into the kitchen with a big basket of laundry. Mike pulled out one of his T-shirts. "If that dog is a rescue dog," he said, laughing, "I'll eat my dirty T-shirt."

At the Fire Station, Station Officer Steele was supervising Sam, Penny and Elvis in an equipment check.

"Now, the whole point of an equipment check," Station Officer Steele told them, "is to examine all the equipment carefully for wear and tear ..."

Just then, a horn tooted outside the Fire Station.

BEEP!

"That must be Mike," said Elvis. "He's come to fix the blocked drain in the kitchen."

Mike and Mandy jumped out of the van. Sam and Radar came over to greet them.

"Sam, is Radar really a rescue dog?" Mandy asked as she patted the dog on the head. She was determined to prove her dad wrong.

"Of course. He has an excellent sense of smell," Sam told her, "so he makes a great sniffer dog!"

This gave Mandy an idea. "Thanks, Sam!" she said, running off.

Elvis and Mike were making music in the Fire Station kitchen. Mike used his tools as drumsticks, while Elvis sang into a spoon.

"What are you two up to in here?" Station Officer Steele shouted from the doorway.

"Trying to unblock the drain, Sir," Mike shouted, standing to attention like a soldier.

Station Officer Steele looked into the sink, which was still blocked.

"I suggest you stop making a song and dance about it, and get on with it!" he bellowed at Mike and Elvis.

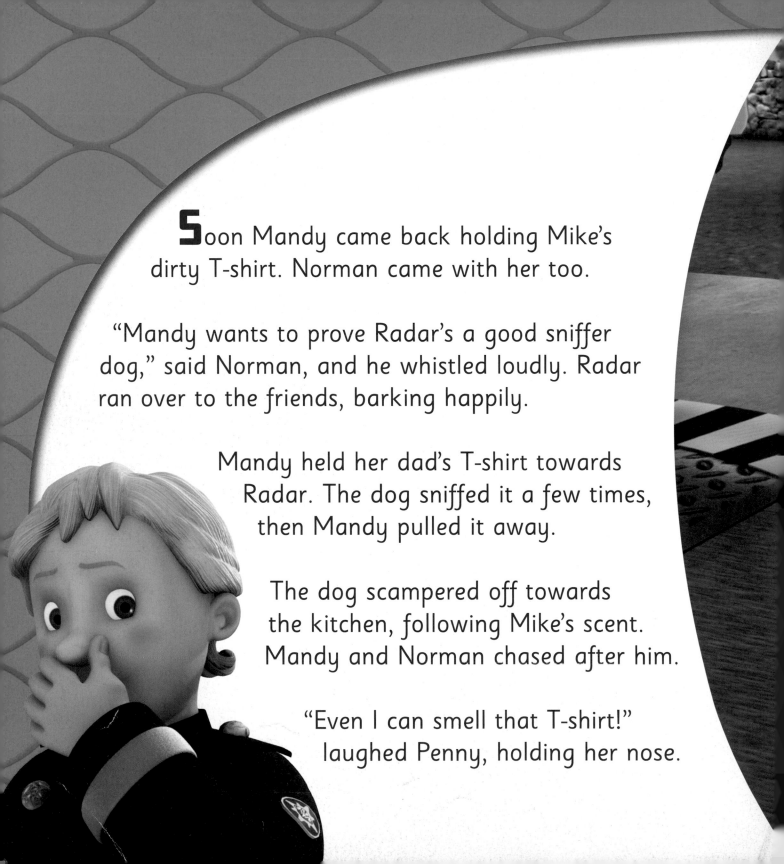

Soon Mandy came back holding Mike's dirty T-shirt. Norman came with her too.

"Mandy wants to prove Radar's a good sniffer dog," said Norman, and he whistled loudly. Radar ran over to the friends, barking happily.

Mandy held her dad's T-shirt towards Radar. The dog sniffed it a few times, then Mandy pulled it away.

The dog scampered off towards the kitchen, following Mike's scent. Mandy and Norman chased after him.

"Even I can smell that T-shirt!" laughed Penny, holding her nose.

Radar burst into the Fire Station kitchen, with Mandy and Norman not far behind.

But Elvis was the only person in the kitchen. "Hello, Mandy," said Elvis, as Radar sniffed around the floor.

"Where's my dad?" Mandy asked.

"He unblocked the drain but he had other jobs to do," Elvis told her.

Suddenly, Radar turned around and scampered out of the kitchen again. He had picked up Mike's scent in a different direction!

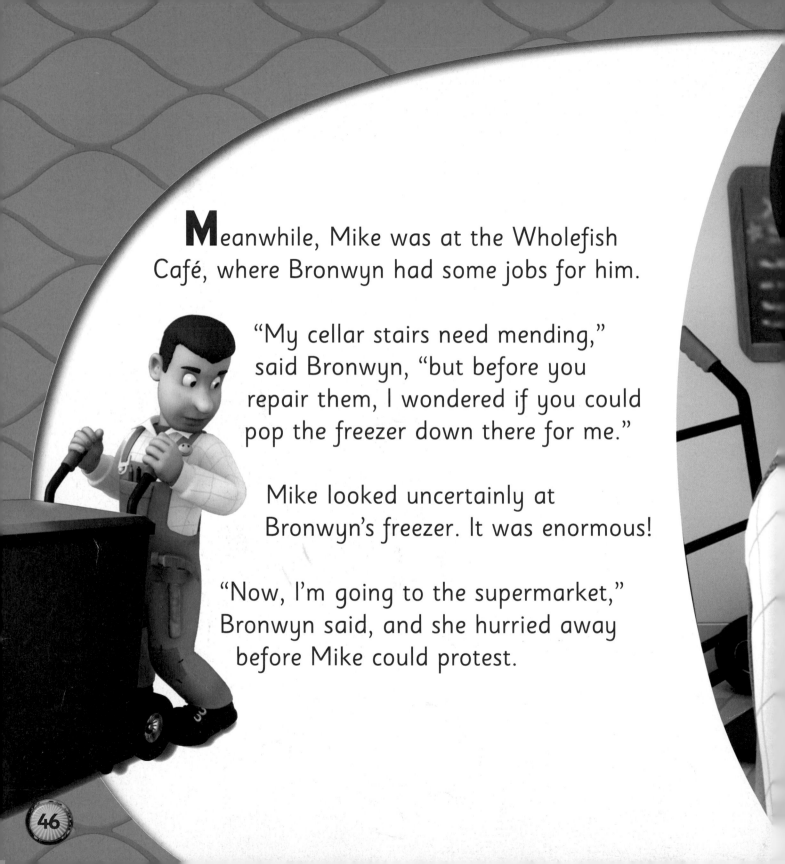

Meanwhile, Mike was at the Wholefish Café, where Bronwyn had some jobs for him.

"My cellar stairs need mending," said Bronwyn, "but before you repair them, I wondered if you could pop the freezer down there for me."

Mike looked uncertainly at Bronwyn's freezer. It was enormous!

"Now, I'm going to the supermarket," Bronwyn said, and she hurried away before Mike could protest.

"Oh dear," sighed Mike, looking at the heavy freezer. Carefully, he loaded it onto a trolley and pulled it towards the cellar door ...

Peering into the darkness, Mike stepped back on to the top step, pulling the trolley after him.

Suddenly, he heard a long, loud **CREAK!**

The cellar stairs collapsed beneath his feet. "Gaaaaaaah!" Mike cried, as he fell down, down, to the hard cellar floor.

He landed – **PHLUNK** – with the freezer right on top of him!

Radar raced through Pontypandy. Finally, he stopped outside Bronwyn's café.

Mandy and Norman arrived soon after, both out of breath.

"Dad was right. Radar's not a rescue dog. He doesn't know where he's going," Mandy said sadly as she stood outside the empty café. "We'd better go back to the Fire Station."

But Radar was whimpering and scratching at the door with his paw.

Suddenly, Mandy spotted a familiar van, parked not far away. "That's Dad's van!" she cried.

As soon as Norman pushed the café door open, Radar ran straight to the top of the cellar stairs ... but the stairs had gone!

Mandy and Norman raced in after Radar and peered down into the darkness. Mandy could see her poor dad trapped under the enormous freezer!

"Dad!" she cried. "Are you all right?"

Mike gave a loud, painful groan.

"I'll phone Fireman Sam," shouted Norman.

"Well done, Radar," gasped Mandy, patting Radar proudly. "You followed Dad's scent after all!"

At the Fire Station, Station Officer Steele read Norman's emergency message.

"Mike Flood's had an accident!" he called out. "He's trapped at the Wholefish Café." He pushed the button to sound the alarm.

Sam, Penny and Elvis slid down the pole and loaded the stretcher and the stair chair into Jupiter.

"We'd better radio Nurse Flood," said Sam.

"OK," said Penny, and she picked up the two-way radio to call Helen.

In no time, they were on their way to the café, and soon after Nurse Flood arrived in her mini-ambulance.

Sam lowered himself into the cellar on a rope.

"Take it easy, Mike," he said. "We'll soon have you out of here."

Nurse Flood peered into the cellar. "Be careful, Sam," she warned. "Don't move him. We need to keep him still in case he's hurt his back."

Sam understood. Carefully he moved the freezer away from Mike without hurting him.

"We'll need the stretcher," said Sam.

Elvis fetched the stretcher basket and lowered it through the cellar door to Sam.

Once Sam was happy that Mike had not hurt his back, he slid the stretcher under Mike and strapped him on safely. Then Penny and Elvis pulled the stretcher basket up to the shop floor.

"Easy does it, now," Sam said, calmly.

The fire crew helped Nurse Flood to lift Mike carefully into the mini-ambulance, and Mandy watched as her mum drove away to the hospital.

"Don't worry, Mandy," said Sam, "your dad will be right as rain."

Before very long, Mike was home, safe and well, with only a broken arm and some bumps and bruises!

Elvis and Sam went to the Floods' house to visit him, and Elvis even took a bunch of flowers.

"How kind of you to come!" said Nurse Flood with a smile, as she took Sam and Elvis through to the living room. "The break in his arm is not too bad, really. He should be back on his feet in no time."

Mike was sitting on the sofa, his arm in a plaster cast. He was very pleased to see Sam and Elvis.

Then in dashed Radar, who immediately ran to Mike to give him lots of doggy kisses!

"Get that silly dog off me!" spluttered Mike.

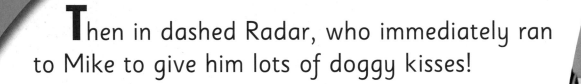

"That silly rescue dog, Dad!" Mandy corrected him. Mike sighed.

"OK, he's a rescue dog. You were right, Mandy!" said Mike, smiling.

"He's a good rockin' doggy!" sang Elvis, using the bunch of flowers as a microphone. "Ooh, yeah, a good rockin' doggy!"

And Radar the rescue dog began to howl along with Elvis!

PLANE CRAZY

One morning, Norman Price was busy at his new hobby – making paper aeroplanes!

He had a special book that told him what to do, and he was following the instructions carefully.

"Fold along lines E to F and G to H," he read, folding his latest plane's wingtips. "There we are!"

Proudly, he held up his plane, then reached for one he had made earlier.

"Flying ace Norman Price is ready to take to the skies!" he beamed, admiring his paper planes.

A little while later, Fireman Sam and Station Officer Steele arrived at the shop.

Norman opened a window. "Fireman Sam! Watch this!" he called, waving one of his planes.

"We haven't got time for any silliness, Norman! Today is Fire Prevention Day," said Station Officer Steele gruffly.

Dilys opened the shop door. "Come in, Station Officer Steele. Never mind my Norman!" she said, waving the fire officers into the shop.

Sam looked up at Norman. "Sorry, Norman. Maybe you can show me your planes some other time."

Sam put a stepladder under the smoke alarm. "We need to check and make sure the supermarket is fire-safe," he told Dilys.

Sam pressed the button on the smoke alarm. It made a loud **BEEP**, which meant it was working properly!

As Sam climbed down the ladder a paper plane whooshed past him! "What was that?" Sam gasped.

"A bat!" shrieked Dilys. "And it's caught in my hair!"

Station Officer Steele plucked the plane out of Dilys' hair. "Norman Price!" he barked, knowing who was to blame.

Norman ran out of the shop to hide. "Station Officer Steele is no fun at all!" he grumbled. He set off for the Floods' house. Mike was in his workshop, hammering a wooden frame together. He didn't see Norman hiding in the doorway until ...

WHOOSH! A paper plane flew right past Mike's face!

Mike looked up as he swung the hammer, and – **BAM!** He hit his thumb!

"Ow!" he yelled, sucking his thumb and staring at the plane. "Where on earth did that come from?"

Norman heard a familiar voice shout, "Norman Price!"

He turned from the workshop doorway to see Station Officer Steele marching towards him, with Sam not far behind. They had come to inspect Mike's workshop to make sure it was fire-safe, too.

Station Officer Steele looked rather angry.

"Not him again!" Norman groaned, and slipped past the Station Officer before he could get another telling off!

Norman trudged off down the road, feeling very fed up.

"I thought it was Fire Prevention Day, not Follow Norman Price Day," he sulked. "But I know one place I won't bump into Station Officer Steele!"

Norman raced over to the Fire Station.

"Whoever heard of preventing fires at a Fire Station?" he sniggered to himself as he tiptoed in.

Norman quickly found a spare piece of paper and made himself another aeroplane. Slowly, he crept to the Fire Station kitchen. Through a gap in the door, he saw Elvis chopping vegetables and singing:

"A-chop-bop potato-bop, I love stew!
A slip-slop-a-peely-pop, yes, I dooooo!"

Norman launched his plane. He watched it fly over Elvis' head and turn a loop-the-loop.

That got Elvis' attention! He looked around and saw Norman looking worried. Where had that plane landed?

"**W**hy are you in my kitchen, Norman Price?" asked Elvis, slicing some carrots.

"No reason," Norman muttered guiltily, lifting things off the counter and peering under them.

Elvis tutted. "I know exactly what you're up to!"

Norman looked up at Elvis in surprise. "You do?"

"Yes! I know how much you like carrots! Out of my kitchen!" Elvis laughed, waving Norman away.

Elvis put his ingredients into the big stew pot on the oven hob, and turned on the heat.

He didn't notice the edges of a paper plane begin to singe and smoulder.

Elvis came out to meet Fireman Sam and Station Officer Steele as Jupiter returned to the Fire Station.

"I trust dinner isn't burnt, Cridlington!" said Station Officer Steele as he wandered off to his office. He opened his office door – and a paper plane flew straight at him! He reached out and caught it mid-air.

"Norman Price!" Station Officer Steele bellowed. Norman ran out of the office and out of sight.

Station Officer Steele looked at the paper plane in his hand. "Hmm!" he said, admiringly. "Not a bad little plane!"

Fireman Sam saw Norman dash across the Fire Station yard and called to him. "Norman! How are you getting on with your paper aeroplanes?"

Norman stared at his feet. "Terribly!" he sighed. "Nobody in Pontypandy likes paper planes."

Meanwhile, Elvis had gone back to the kitchen to check on the stew.

"Great balls of fire!" he cried.

A fire had spread across the kitchen counter!

"Fire! Fire!" cried Elvis.

In his office, Station Officer Steele heard Elvis shouting.

"Fire in the Fire Station kitchen!" he cried, hitting the alarm button.

Sam rushed back inside the Fire Station, and bumped into Elvis, as he sped down the stairs.

"Sam! Sam! The kitchen's on fire!" shouted Elvis, and they dashed to put on their equipment.

Norman watched the fire officers rushing about, and felt very guilty indeed.

Fireman Sam ran into the kitchen, with Elvis not far behind.

"Cut the gas supply, Elvis," Sam called, and Elvis switched off the cooker.

Sam spotted a fire extinguisher, and immediately began to spray foam over the flames.

HISS!

The flames soon died down. Sam had the fire under control.

"What about my stew?" cried Elvis.

Sam lifted the lid of the stew pot. Smoke drifted out.

"You've overcooked dinner before, Elvis," he laughed, "but never that badly!"

"Firemen are supposed to put out fires, Cridlington, not start them!" said Station Officer Steele.

Sam pulled a scrap of paper from the hob.

"It's a paper aeroplane," said Elvis.

"Norman Price!" said Station Officer Steele, turning to see Norman cowering behind him.

"Sorry!" Norman whimpered. "It was an accident!"

Station Officer Steele cleared his throat. "Perhaps I should have a word with the lad, Sam," he said. "Set him on the straight and narrow, as it were ..."

"Don't be too hard on Norman, Sir," said Elvis.

As Station Officer Steele led Norman out of the kitchen, Sam saw a fresh paper plane in the Station Officer's hand.

In his office, Station Officer Steele certainly had some wise words for Norman.

"The first rule of paper aeroplanes," he said, "is to be careful where you throw them ... Now, watch this loop-the-loop!"

THE HERO NEXT DOOR

After finishing his last job at the Pontypandy Fire Station, Sam put away his fire helmet and said goodbye to Penny.

"What will you do today, now that you're off duty?" Penny asked.

"I have some chores to do at home," he smiled. "But first, I'm off to the supermarket. See you tomorrow!"

Whistling cheerfully, Sam headed into town.

At the supermarket, Mike the handyman was finishing a job, too. "There, that's better," he said, as he put cement over a crack in the paving behind the shop.

"Thank you," Dilys said, and went to step on the cement.

"Whoa!" said Mike, holding her back. "The cement needs time to set first."

When Mike and Dilys had gone, naughty Norman looked at the wet cement, thinking of a very naughty idea ...

At the front of the supermarket, Mike climbed up his ladder to fix a leak in the roof.

When Sam arrived, Dilys knew he was off duty as he wasn't wearing his helmet. "How are you spending your time off?" she asked.

"I've lots to do. I need to weed my garden, then iron some clothes and paint my front door. But first, I have to buy some things from your shop," Sam explained.

"Come inside!" Dilys smiled.

Meanwhile, Norman found a long stick to draw pictures in the wet cement. Just then, his friend Sarah walked by with her dog, Nipper.

"Want to see something really cool round the back?" Norman asked her.

"Sure!" said Sarah. She tied her dog's lead to Mike's ladder. "Wait here, Nipper. I'll be back soon!" she told him.

Nipper sat on the pavement. Then he spotted Lion the cat walking past.

"Woof!" barked Nipper.

"Meow!" Lion yowled, then he ran across the road.

Nipper bounded after Lion, but his lead was still tied to Mike's ladder. The ladder crashed to the ground, leaving Mike hanging from the roof!

"Argh!" shouted Mike. **"HELP!"**

Inside the shop, Dilys was showing Sam a new iron. They heard Mike's shouts and Sam ran outside. Dilys rushed out too, forgetting to turn off the iron.

"Great Fires of London!" Sam cried. "Hang on, Mike. I'll get the ladder."

He saw Nipper dragging the ladder across the road just as Trevor's bus appeared. Slamming on the brakes, Trevor stopped just in time!

"Well done, Trevor!" called Sam, as he untied Nipper. Just as Mike was about to fall, Sam put up the ladder and saved him!

Trevor jumped out of his bus to bring Nipper off the road. "Are you all right?" he asked Mike.

"Yes, thanks to Sam," Mike answered. "I'm lucky he was here."

Sam smiled. But suddenly, Trevor's bus began to roll down the street, with no driver inside!

"Watch out!" Dilys cried.

"Oh no, I must have left the handbrake off!" cried Trevor.

"**S**tand back!" called Sam as he chased after the bus. The situation was very dangerous – especially if someone was in the path of the runaway bus!

Sam ran as fast as he could to the bus' door. Just as it was about to crash into a house, he jumped into the driver's seat and yanked on the handbrake. The bus jolted to a stop, just a few centimetres from the front door!

"Sam, you saved the day – again!" cheered Trevor.

As Sam was catching his breath, he heard more shouts coming from behind the supermarket.

"Help, I'm stuck!"

Dilys cried, "That sounds like Norman!"

Sam dashed around the back of the supermarket, with the others following after him.

Norman had been drawing a picture in the wet cement, but his trainers were stuck now that it was set! "Help! I can't move my feet!" he wailed.

Sam said, "I'll get you out, Norman."
He pulled Norman up until he popped free.

"Norman Price, what am I going to do with you?" scolded Dilys.

"Sorry, Mam," Norman said. "Thank you for saving me, Fireman Sam," he added.

Dilys went on. "All I ask is a little peace and qui—"

BEEP! BEEP! BEEP!

Suddenly, a loud alarm went off nearby!

"That sounds like the supermarket's smoke alarm," said Sam.

Dilys gasped. "I must have forgotten to turn the iron off. I'll run in and call 999!"

But Sam stopped her. "Never enter a burning building," he told Dilys. "I'll run back to the station and get help."

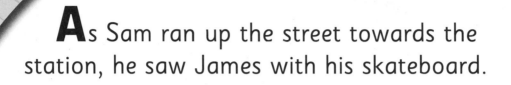

As Sam ran up the street towards the station, he saw James with his skateboard.

"Hi, Sam," smiled James. "I was just – **oh!**"

Before James could finish, Sam grabbed the skateboard and jumped onto it, whizzing up the road. "Sorry, James!" he called. "It's an emergency! I'll bring it right back."

Once at the station, Sam and the crew rushed out in Jupiter, with its sirens wailing.

Nee nah!
Nee nah!

Jupiter screeched to a stop in front of the supermarket and the fire crew jumped out.

"Elvis, shut off the power in the building," Sam ordered. "Penny and I will work the fire hose."

"Yes, sir!" Elvis saluted before he ran off.

Sam and Penny unrolled Jupiter's water hose and turned on the tap. Inside the supermarket, they sprayed the fire with water. They soon put the fire out. Luckily, no one was hurt!

A short time later, Penny asked, "Did you get all your jobs done on your day off, Sam?"

"No ... but I've certainly been busy!" Sam laughed.

"We're lucky you were here," Dilys told him. "And since you gave up your day off to help all of us, I'll do your ironing and Mike will paint your door. And, Norman will weed your garden for the rest of the summer!"

"Aw, Mam ..." Norman whinged.

"Thanks, everyone," said Sam.

Sam finally headed home after his busy day, but he didn't get far before he heard more cries for help.

"Arrrrgh! I can't stop! **HELP!**" Station Officer Steele came flying down the street on James' skateboard. The skateboard was out of control, but Steele was going too fast to stop!

"Don't worry, sir! I'll save you!" Sam called out as he started to give chase.

As everyone laughed, Elvis joked, "Well, as Sam always says, a good firefighter is never off duty!"

THE GREAT FIRE OF PONTYPANDY

It was a special day in Pontypandy.

Chief Fire Officer Boyce had come all the way from Newtown to give Fireman Sam a medal for bravery. "Well done, Sam!" he said.

"Thank you, sir!" replied Sam.

Station Officer Steele and the rest of the fire crew were very proud of Sam. He was a hero!

After the ceremony, Chief Fire Officer Boyce asked Sam to be the Station Officer in Newtown.

"I need to think about it," Sam replied. He wasn't sure he wanted to leave Pontypandy.

Later, Sam, Elvis and Radar went to the forest. They put up signs to remind people not to light campfires.

With the weather so hot and dry, a forest fire could spread quickly. Pontypandy would be in great danger!

Before Sam returned to the Fire Station, Elvis asked him, "I'd like to be a hero too. How do you do it?"

"I'm not sure, Elvis," Sam replied with surprise. "I just try to be the best firefighter I can be."

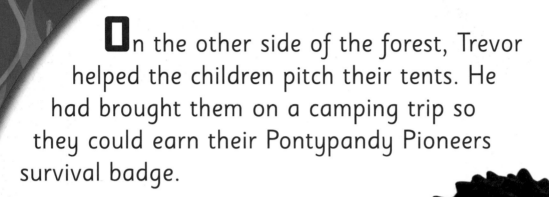

On the other side of the forest, Trevor helped the children pitch their tents. He had brought them on a camping trip so they could earn their Pontypandy Pioneers survival badge.

Their next task was to gather food from the forest for lunch, but all they could find were a few blackberries. The Pioneers were hungry!

Trevor tried to lead a singsong, but the children were too grumpy to sing. Earning the survival badge was hard work!

Norman and his cousin Derek had secretly brought some sausages on the trip. They sneaked away to find a place to cook them.

"But there are no fires allowed," Derek said.

"We can't eat raw sausages, can we!" Norman replied as he rubbed two sticks together.

"Norman!" It was his mum, Dilys! The boys left the sticks and ran back to the camp. Suddenly, the sticks burst into flames!

At the Mountain Rescue Station,
Tom Thomas looked out of the window.
He spotted a strange cloud over the woods
and looked closer.

It wasn't a cloud, it was smoke from a fire!
Tom called the Fire Station straight away.

"Tom here. I see smoke in the forest,"
he reported to Station Officer Steele.
"I'll try to put out the fire before it
spreads!"

With Sam gone, Elvis put up the last of the signs. Suddenly, Elvis' walkie-talkie crackled.

"Cridlington!" shouted Station Officer Steele. "A forest fire has started and there are people on the camp site. You must get them out of danger!"

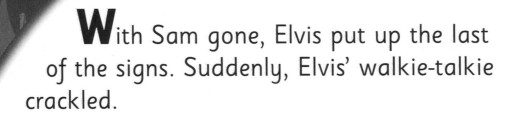

"You can count on me, sir!" Elvis said. "Let's go, Radar!"

Tom flew Wallaby One over the forest and dropped an enormous bucket of water onto the flames.

"Tom," Sam said over the walkie-talkie. "How does it look?"

"Not good, Sam," answered Tom. "The wind is blowing the fire towards Pontypandy!"

"We'll be right there to tackle it from the ground," promised Sam.

With lights flashing and sirens wailing, Jupiter and Venus sped to the forest.

Sam, Penny and Station Officer Steele sprayed water on the trees and grass. They hoped that it would stop the flames.

If the fire spread, Pontypandy could be destroyed. It was up to Sam and the crew to save the town!

"Steady now!" called Sam. Fighting this fire would take a lot of teamwork!

Meanwhile, Elvis asked Radar to sniff around the forest. With his clever nose, Radar soon led Elvis right to the campers!

Elvis was happy to find everyone safe, but the thick smoke was making it hard to breathe.

"Follow me!" said Elvis. He heard Jupiter's siren and led the group towards the sound. Finally, they found their way out of the smoky woods.

"Well done, Elvis!" said Sam.

Elvis joined the fire crew battling the blaze, but it was too strong for the water hoses.

CRACK! Suddenly, a burning branch broke off from a tree and fell straight towards Sam!

Without thinking, Elvis knocked right into Sam and rolled him to safety. The branch landed on the spot where Sam had been standing.

"Thanks, Elvis!" cried Sam. "You saved my life!"

Despite the crew's hard work, the fire was still heading straight for Pontypandy.

"We must get everyone to safety!" called Station Officer Steele.

The fire crew took the townspeople and their pets to the harbour and helped them on board Charlie's fishing boat. As they watched the fire creep towards Pontypandy, Sarah asked, "Why are we going out onto the water, Dad?"

"It's the only place where the fire can't reach us," said Charlie.

As the fire got closer, Sam felt very sad. He didn't want to see Pontypandy destroyed.

Just then, a drop of water fell on his nose. Sam looked up at the clouds. "It's raining!" he shouted.

"Let's hope it's enough to put out the fire!" said Penny as the rain began to pour down.

Tom soon radioed from his helicopter. "The rain has put out the fire. We're out of danger!"

The townspeople cheered as the boat returned to the dock. Pontypandy was safe!

Soon after, there was another medal ceremony at Pontypandy Fire Station.

"Elvis, you showed real bravery during the Great Fire," Boyce said. "Well done!"

Elvis saluted. Now he was a hero, too!

"And it's my pleasure to give survival badges to the Pontypandy Pioneers," Trevor Evans said next. "Well, to most of them …"

"This is all your fault!" Norman and Derek moaned to each other. There were no badges for them!

Afterwards, Sam told Chief Fire Officer Boyce that he had decided not to take the job in Newtown.

"Why didn't you take it, Sam?" Elvis asked him later. "You could have been a Station Officer in Newtown with your very own crew."

Fireman Sam smiled. "I learned a lot during the Great Fire, Elvis," he said. "I almost lost Pontypandy and now I know I never want to leave. Pontypandy will always be my home!"

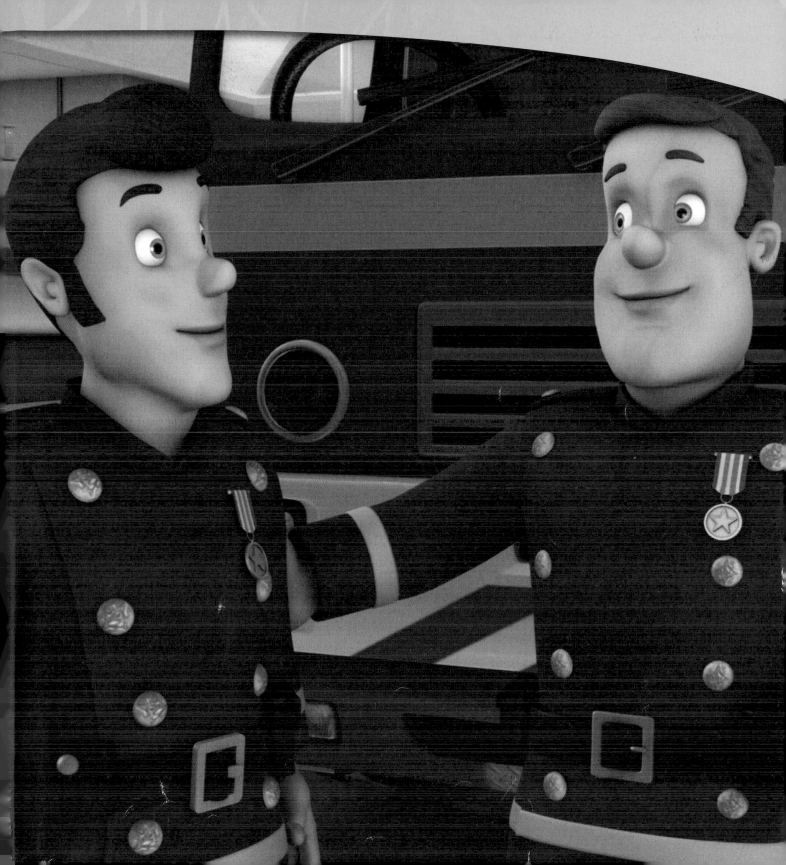